This book belongs to:

....

MR WALKER

and the Perfect Mess

For Holly and Catriona – JB

For Wendy Walker – SA

PUFFIN BOOKS

UK | USA | Canada | Ireland | Australia
India | New Zealand | South Africa | China

Penguin Random House Australia is part of the Penguin Random House group of companies whose addresses can be found at global.penguinrandomhouse.com

First published by Puffin Books, an imprint of Penguin Random House Australia Pty Ltd, in 2019

Cover background © Asya Alexandrova/Shutterstock.com
Cover design by Kirby Armstrong © Penguin Random House Australia Pty Ltd
Internal design by Midland Typesetters © Penguin Random House Australia Pty Ltd
Typeset by Midland Typesetters, Australia

Printed and bound in China

A catalogue record for this book is available from the National Library of Australia

ISBN 978 0 14 379311 3 (Hardback)

penguin.com.au

MR WALKER
and the Perfect Mess

JESS BLACK
Illustrated by Sara Acton

PUFFIN BOOKS

CHAPTER ONE

It was the first morning of December and Mr Walker had been swept up in the festive cheer. He had little choice. The Reeves household was crackers about Christmas! After breakfast, they gathered around an object that was the size of a large cereal box. It was made of cardboard and on its front was a Christmas tree.

Mr Walker cocked his head to one side. *It must be a teeny-tiny tree to fit in such a small box*, he thought. *How will we hang all the decorations on it?*

'This is an advent calendar,' Mrs Reeves explained. 'We use it to count down the days until Christmas.'

'Inside each window is chocolate,' Sophie added excitedly.

How curious, thought Mr Walker. He gave the cardboard windows a sniff.

'Not this time,' said Mrs Reeves. 'This is an extra-special advent calendar.'

Without the promise of chocolate, Sophie doubted that very much.

'Lollies?' Amanda asked hopefully.

'Why don't we open a window and find out?' Mrs Reeves suggested.

The girls sighed with disappointment. That *definitely* meant there were no lollies.

'Who would like to go first?' Henry asked.

'Me!' both girls replied at exactly the same moment.

Mrs Reeves laughed. 'How about we take it in turns? Amanda can open today's window and Sophie can open the next one tomorrow.'

Mr Walker's tail wagged from side to side. *And I'll have my turn the day after that.*

'Goody!' cried Amanda. She reached forward and gently opened the delicate cardboard door with the number one on it.

Mr Walker inched closer to take a look.

'What is it?' Sophie asked, peering over her younger sister's shoulder.

Amanda held up the tiny ornament for the others to see. 'It's an angel,' she gushed, marvelling at the porcelain figurine. Attached to it was a loop of fine gold thread.

'Time to get ready for school now,' Mrs Reeves informed the girls.

Amanda placed the figurine carefully on the sideboard, where it would be joined by lots of other Christmas-tree ornaments over the next three and a half weeks. The girls then vanished into their bedrooms to get dressed for school while Henry and Mrs Reeves cleared the breakfast table. Mr Walker tidied his bed, making sure to tuck his wombat toy under his blanket.

'Has anyone seen my school hat?' Sophie called out.

I have! Mr Walker trotted over to the couch and plucked the rather sorry-looking sunhat out from behind a cushion.

Amanda burst into the room, wide-eyed with panic. 'I can't find my reader!'

Luckily, Mr Walker knew exactly where it was. He padded to Amanda's room and pulled the reader out from under her bed. Problem solved.

'What would we do without you?'
Mrs Reeves said, giving him a pat and
a treat. 'Now, perhaps you can help that
husband of mine? He's running a little
late this morning.'

Mr Walker was glad to be of help. He
spied Henry's tie and freshly polished
shoes and took them to find their owner.
He followed the scent of Henry's woody
aftershave into the kitchen and was
delighted to find Henry and Mrs Reeves
dancing.

'On the first day of Christmas my true
love gave to me a croissant and a cup of
black tea!' Henry sang. He took Mrs Reeves
by the hand and spun her around.

Mrs Reeves laughed. 'On the second day
of Christmas my true love gave to me two
breakfast plates, a croissant and a cup of
black tea!' she sang, handing Henry
two clean dishes to dry and put away.

What fun! Mr Walker thought, his tail wagging to the beat.

Sophie marched into the kitchen to collect her lunch box. 'On the third day of Christmas my true love gave to me . . .' She searched the countertop and picked up three red-and-white-striped sweets. 'Three candy canes, two breakfast plates and a croissant and a cup of black tea!' she sang at the top of her lungs.

'My turn!' Amanda shouted, scooting into the kitchen with her teddy bear held high. 'On the fourth day of Christmas my true love gave to me four teddy bears, three candy canes, two breakfast plates and a croissant and a cup of black tea!' she trilled while skipping around in circles with Sophie.

Mr Walker danced along with them, having a whale of a time. *On the fifth day of Christmas my true love gave to me*

five meaty bones, four special treats, three back rubs, two tummy tickles and a squeaky toy shaped like a Christmas tree!

Before the Reeves family had reached the twelfth day of Christmas, they had all dissolved into fits of giggles.

'Grab a frozen juice box each,' Mrs Reeves said to the girls as she wiped away tears of laughter. 'It's going to be hot again today.'

'Make sure you drink lots of water,' Sophie said to Mr Walker.

Good idea, Sophie! Mr Walker rewarded the girl with a sloppy kiss. It had been awfully hot on his morning walks lately; he dreaded to think what the rest of the summer had in store.

Despite that, Mr Walker was looking forward to the holidays. He had an inkling this was going to be the best Christmas ever, and certainly the most special, as it would be groundskeeper Josephine's last at Park Hyatt. He especially couldn't wait for all the scrumptious food, such as honey-glazed ham, potato salad and – best of all – pudding! His stomach rumbled at the thought.

'Ready for work, Mr Walker?' Henry asked, straightening his tie.

Mr Walker's whiskers twitched with excitement. *As ready as I'll ever be!*

CHAPTER TWO

As Mr Walker went about his morning rounds, it was hard not to be reminded of all the precious moments he had shared with Josephine. Memories lay in wait at every turn. He stepped out into the garden courtyard and recalled how she had taught him to dig holes for bulbs. He had made an awful mess at first but now had it down to a fine art. He chortled to himself, remembering the countless games of fetch and tug-of-war he and Josephine had enjoyed over an old red gardening glove. He had let her win on a few occasions, although he'd never let on.

Mr Walker padded to the front desk and sank to the ground. The morning's festive cheer had floated away bit by bit, leaving him with the realisation that he was going to miss his friend Josephine very much. He rested his snout on the marble floor between his paws and sighed. He was so sad that he didn't even get up to lick the splotches of ice-cream a little boy had left in his wake.

Omid peered down at Mr Walker. 'I too am finding it difficult to focus on my tasks this morning,' he admitted. 'It is a bittersweet time here at Park Hyatt.'

Bittersweet? Mr Walker licked his lips. *Like a key-lime pie or a lemon cheesecake with too much lemon?*

Omid noticed that Mr Walker was staring at him intently. 'A bittersweet feeling is when you're sad and happy at the same time,' he explained. 'Even though it's hard for us to say goodbye to Josephine, we should be happy for her to have such an exciting opportunity.'

Happy? Mr Walker frowned. *How can I be happy that my friend is leaving?*

Omid went back to his papers and sighed.

Thomas the porter trudged past, looking uncharacteristically glum.

Henry stepped out of his office and took note of all their sad faces. 'Come now, everyone, is this how you want Josephine to remember us? She deserves our brightest smiles and our best wishes so that she has a wonderful send-off.'

13

Henry is right, thought Mr Walker. *Josephine always has an encouraging word and a ready smile for those in need of one.* He sat up straight and, taking a deep breath, resolved to spend as much time with Josephine as he could. They still had a week to share more happy moments to look back on fondly.

'Let's squeeze in a meeting to discuss her gift,' Henry said, checking the time. 'Quick, before she walks past and suspects anything.'

A surprise for Josephine. What fun! Mr Walker thought back to the advent calendar and leapt to his feet. He had an idea for the perfect farewell present for Josephine! *But how to tell Henry?* he wondered. *I know!*

Mr Walker poked his head inside Henry's office and saw the array of Christmas cards displayed on his desk. They were all variations of red, green and gold, with prancing reindeer, chimney-climbing Santas, snowy vistas and . . .

There it is – the Christmas tree! He delicately plucked the card from the rest. It had travelled all the way from the other side of the world. With his prized

possession in tow, Mr Walker trotted out of the office to join the others. Meraj, Monica, Omid, Elvis, Chef Remy and Thomas were huddled around Henry at the front desk.

'We have the Guide Dogs fundraiser tomorrow to keep us busy,' said Henry. 'There will be a big marquee set up on the lawn as well as refreshments and live music. You all know your various responsibilities, but do give me a shout if you need anything.'

When he was a puppy, Mr Walker had trained to be a Guide Dog. He knew he'd be seeing lots of old friends, both human and canine, at the lunch. He couldn't wait to show them around his hotel and introduce them to the Reeves family and his friends on staff.

'In addition to the fundraiser, we have our regular Christmas guests arriving, so we're fully booked until early January,' Henry continued. 'The extreme heat we've been experiencing is another cause for concern as the forecast for the next few days is off the charts, but we will persevere and try our best. Now, on to Josephine's farewell gift. Has anyone had any ideas?'

Yes, I have! Mr Walker was panting excitedly while his tail *whump*, *whump*, *whumped* on the floor. He nudged Henry's leg and held the card out to him.

'What's this?' Henry asked, taking it from Mr Walker. He opened it and smiled. 'Oh, it's Mr Feldman's card. Yes, it was such a lovely sentiment. I think Mr Walker wants us to write a nice message to Josephine. Of course we will.'

Yes, but that's not all. Mr Walker pawed at the card.

'How about something to do with the garden?' Elvis suggested.

Mr Walker sat down and gave a small whine. Why was nobody listening to him?

'Or for the farmhouse,' Meraj said. 'I know Josephine plans to make lots of changes to it.'

Mr Walker ran around in circles, three to be precise.

'I think we should do something really special here too, though,' Omid added.

Mr Walker yipped in agreement.

'There's an idea. What would Josephine find special?' Henry said, looking around for inspiration.

Mr Walker nudged the card in Henry's hand and let out a bark. Everyone turned to look at him. It was common knowledge that Mr Walker never raised his voice. Whatever he had to say must be very important.

Henry picked up the card and took a closer look at it. After a pause, his eyes lit up. 'I'm sorry I didn't understand at first, Mr Walker, but you've had a most excellent idea. I love it!'

Mr Walker beamed. *Hooray!*

Elvis cleared his throat. 'Care to share it with the rest of us?'

'Oh, of course.' Henry grinned. 'Mr Walker has proposed we have a real tree this year, which we can give to Josephine as a gift for her new home.'

There were murmurs of appreciation.

'Nothing compares to the smell of fresh pine,' Meraj said dreamily.

Monica clapped her hands. 'Each staff member could make a decoration for her tree. They could write messages too and hang them from the branches.'

'That's a terrific idea!' Henry exclaimed.

While everyone was discussing the present, Mr Walker spied Josephine heading straight for them. *Uh-oh!*

He had to do something, but what? There was nothing else for it. Mr Walker bounded across the marble floor, dodging guests and suitcases, and skidded straight into Josephine's legs.

'Ooh!' Josephine's arms turned like windmills.

She managed to catch her balance just in time. 'Goodness, I didn't see you there, Mr Walker.'

The others looked over at the commotion and panicked. By the time Mr Walker and Josephine made their way to the front desk, everyone but Omid had skedaddled.

'Hello,' Josephine said, flashing Omid a big smile. 'I've come to tell you that my replacement, Haru, starts tomorrow. Can you let me know when he arrives?'

'Absolutely. Yes, indeedy. I will make sure to do that,' Omid said, shuffling the pile of papers in front of him.

'Thank you.' Josephine looked at him curiously. 'Is everything all right?'

Omid nodded. 'Mhmm, nothing out of the ordinary whatsoever.'

'Okay then.' Josephine shrugged and winked at Mr Walker. 'Have a lovely afternoon, you two.'

Mr Walker and Omid let out a sigh of relief. That had been a close call. A very close call indeed.

CHAPTER THREE

Now that the staff had agreed on a gift for Josephine, it was all paws on deck as there was plenty to do in preparation for the Guide Dogs event. Henry and Mr Walker ventured outside to see how they could be of help.

Mr Walker wondered what he could give Josephine. He wanted it to be extra special but wasn't sure what it could be. As they trotted past the vegetable and fruit garden, he noticed the strawberry patch was full of the red fruit. *Mmmm, Josephine makes the best strawberry jam.* Mr Walker sighed. All thoughts seemed to lead him back to Josephine.

They turned the corner and found her already hard at work, placing shade cloths over the most fragile plants. She spotted them and waved. 'Hi there!' she called.

Mr Walker bounded over and gave her a hug.

Josephine threw her head back and laughed. 'That's the second time today you've bowled me over, but I'm happy to see you too and am grateful for the help.'

'I'm afraid your last few days here will be very busy,' said Henry, catching up to them.

'No need to worry about me,' said Josephine, fanning her face with her sunhat. 'I'm more concerned for my poor petunias. They've completely wilted and, to top it off, the gardenias are dropping like flies.'

'Oh dear. Well, I'll leave you to it then. Just let me know if you need more help,' said Henry. 'Mr Walker, are you coming with me?'

Mr Walker picked up the edge of a shade cloth between his teeth and began to drag it across the lawn. He wanted to spend every available moment by Josephine's side.

'I'll take that as a no.' Henry chuckled and waved goodbye, then headed up the driveway.

Mr Walker and Josephine set to work, making sure that even the most delicate of flowers and shrubs would be protected from the relentless heat. The light shade cloth was easy to handle, and Mr Walker soon became adept at helping to lift it over the plants and hold it still while Josephine staked it into place. Then came time to construct the large marquee for the Guide Dogs event.

'Shall we?' Josephine gestured to a spot under an oak tree.

They sat down and watched as the grounds staff worked like busy bees around a hive. Eventually, the marquee went up. Five pairs of workers tugged at the strong ropes to secure them to the ground.

Josephine wrapped an arm around Mr Walker and pulled him in for a hug. 'You know, my father's decision to retire and pass on the farm to me came as a surprise, but once I thought about it, I realised I was ready for the challenge.' She smiled and gave him a squeeze. 'I'll really miss being here, though. I'll miss you especially.'

Mr Walker touched his nose to her cheek. *I'll miss you too.*

In that moment, he knew exactly what his present would be.

CHAPTER FOUR

Mr Walker and the girls burst into the living room, dripping wet and full of chatter.

'Let's get you dried and changed,' said Mrs Reeves. She sent Sophie and Amanda into the bathroom and gave Mr Walker a rub-down with a large fluffy towel. Although he wasn't allowed in the swimming pool, he had still managed to get quite a bit of water splashed onto his fur.

Once they had changed into fresh clothes, the girls set to work on their Christmas decorations. Spread around them was a mess of coloured paper, cardboard, paint and pots of glitter. Mr Walker was intrigued. He crouched down, catching a whiff of craft glue as the fan swung in his direction.

'We're making paper garlands,' Sophie explained.

It looked like terrific fun. Sophie had looped red and green strips of paper together to form a long chain that could be wound around a Christmas tree or strung up along the walls. Mr Walker was most impressed and wagged his tail with enthusiasm.

'Oops!' squealed Sophie. 'Your tail!'

It seemed Mr Walker had managed to get himself tangled up in the paper chain.

'Here, turn around,' Sophie instructed, trying to free him. Mr Walker did as she bid, but that only seemed to make things worse. His whole body was now wrapped up in the coloured paper.

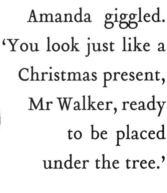

Amanda giggled. 'You look just like a Christmas present, Mr Walker, ready to be placed under the tree.'

'Careful,' Sophie said. 'Try turning the other way.'

Mr Walker moved very slowly so as not to tear the delicate decoration and, with help from the girls, he was soon free.

'Tada!' Sophie held up the garland, which was almost twice as long as she was. 'Where shall I hang it?'

Mr Walker looked around the living room. It was already filled with lots of the girls' artistic creations. Pictures of the family and Mr Walker adorned almost every available surface. His eyes fell on the sideboard. It was the perfect place for the paper garland, draped around the advent calendar and its little ornaments. They now had a reindeer and a sleigh in their collection.

'Good idea, Mr Walker,' said Sophie.

Mrs Reeves entered the room, carrying a plate of watermelon slices. The girls descended on them and were soon slurping and munching away.

'Thanks, Mum!' Sophie said, with juice dribbling down her chin.

'Mum, you know how you can make paper-chain people that hold hands in a line?' Amanda asked. 'I want to make a paper chain of flowers for Josephine.'

'That's a lovely idea, sweetheart,' said Mrs Reeves. 'Why don't you draw the flower and I'll help you fold the paper and cut it?'

'Can we make a paper-chain dog too?' asked Sophie.

'I don't see why not,' said Mrs Reeves. 'How does that sound, Mr Walker? Would you like your very own decoration?'

Mr Walker liked the idea immensely. He wagged his tail, but accidentally collided with the jar full of dirty paint-brushes. *Whoopsie-daisy!*

Mrs Reeves rushed to fetch a tea towel from the kitchen.

'Silly Mr Walker!' Sophie laughed.

Oh dear, oh dear. Mr Walker was in a tizz. He stood in the puddle of water, not knowing what to do with himself. He stepped back and accidentally dipped all four paws in Amanda's paint palette. *Oh no, I've made it worse!*

Mr Walker tried to wipe the paint onto a piece of paper. He hadn't meant to make such a mess. Really, he hadn't.

'Look, Mr Walker's made paw prints on the decorations,' Amanda said, holding up a sheet a paper.

Indeed he had. Mr Walker felt terrible. The girls would be most upset that their decorations had been ruined.

Sophie gasped and threw her arms

around Mr Walker. 'I love it!' she declared, cuddling him.

'What a clever idea,' Amanda agreed.

It turned out that the girls weren't cross at all. In fact, they were pleased.

Would you look at that. Mr Walker's tail *thump*, *thump*, *thumped* on the carpet.

'Can we have a few more, please?' Sophie said, squirting more paint onto her palette.

Mr Walker was only too happy to oblige. His decorations did look quite striking, if he did say so himself!

CHAPTER FIVE

The next day turned out to be even hotter than the one before.

'We just have to keep doing our best to make the guests as comfortable as possible,' Henry said to his staff. 'Luckily, the marquees will provide shade for those outside.'

Mr Walker sniffed the air. The foyer usually smelled of fresh flowers and floor polish, but a new aroma told him that Josephine's tree had arrived.

Oh goodie! thought Mr Walker. He trotted
to the front entrance of the hotel to take
a look and his eyes widened at the sight.
Sure enough, Thomas and Elvis were busy
removing the straps from an absolutely
enormous pine tree. Mr Walker bounded
back over to Henry to share the good news.
He kept a lookout for Josephine. The last
thing they needed was for her to see the
tree and have the surprise spoiled.

'What is it, Mr Walker?' Henry asked.
He looked up to see Thomas waving him
over to the hotel entrance. Henry left to

lend Thomas a hand and before long the three men re-emerged inside the foyer, each with a section of the tree underarm. They hovered by the open doorway.

'Is the coast clear?' Thomas called to Omid.

Omid nodded and hurried out from behind the front desk. 'All clear. Monica, can you hold the lift for us?'

Monica retreated in the direction of the elevator.

'Can you keep a lookout, Mr Walker?' Omid asked.

It would be my honour. Mr Walker stood guard, pleased to be of service. Out of the corner of one eye, he could see the three men tiptoeing into the foyer with the tree. They were almost at the lift when, to his horror, Mr Walker noticed that Josephine was making her way up the grand staircase towards them. *Oh no!*

Mr Walker let out a yip of warning and raced down the stairs.

Henry, Thomas and Elvis froze. All Josephine had to do was look up and she would see them. There was no disguising what they were carrying! Thinking fast on his feet, Mr Walker made a bid to divert her attention. He raced past her to the bottom of the stairs and barked at her to follow him.

'Whatever is the matter, Mr Walker?' Josephine asked, looking puzzled. She turned and skipped down the steps.

Mr Walker bounced up and down on the spot. *Come with me!*

'I do believe the heat has finally got to you,' Josephine said with concern. 'You're acting most peculiarly.'

That's it. Follow me! Mr Walker was so thrilled his plan was working that he felt compelled to run around in circles.

'Thank goodness,' Henry sighed. 'This tree is getting awfully heavy.'

The trio continued across the foyer and had almost reached the lift when Elvis peered over the bannister to the floor below. 'Uh-oh,' he said. 'Something's up.'

Josephine had stopped in her tracks. She slapped her forehead with the palm of her hand. 'Of course!' she exclaimed. 'I see what you're trying to do.'

You do? Mr Walker's heart sank with disappointment. That meant Josephine had guessed what they were up to and the surprise was ruined. Mr Walker wanted to bury his head under his paws. He had failed miserably.

'I'd completely forgotten the plants at the back entrance. They'll need shade right away,' Josephine said, ruffling his velvet ears. 'Thanks for reminding me!'

Mr Walker almost collapsed with relief, but there was work to do. As Josephine made her way outside, he dashed up the stairs to join Henry and the others, who were busy trying to get the pine tree into the lift.

'Well done, Mr Walker!' Thomas puffed.

'Just in the nick of time,' said Elvis. 'This tree is growing heavier by the minute.'

Monica frowned. 'Do you think it will fit?' she asked uncertainly.

'If we angle it just right,' said Henry.

After a bit of manoeuvring and grunting, the tree finally made it inside the lift. They travelled up to the twenty-third floor and squirreled the tree away into a storeroom. Mr Walker took a step back to get a good look at it. The tree was nothing short of majestic, and he couldn't help noticing that the large bucket of soil it was standing in would make the perfect hiding place for his present to Josephine.

Thomas mopped his brow with a linen handkerchief. 'That was a close call.'

'Disaster averted,' Henry said happily.

'Mission accomplished,' agreed Elvis.

'Time to get back to it before anyone wonders where we are,' said Monica.

It was at that moment that the lights in the hall went out.

'That's strange,' said Henry. He pushed the lift button a few times, but it didn't light up.

Monica gasped. 'A power cut!'

'You're kidding,' Elvis said with a groan. 'That's all we need right now.'

Henry shook his head. 'I was afraid this might happen. It was only a matter of time in heat like this. It puts tremendous pressure on the electricity grid.'

Oh dear! Mr Walker turned circles in the dark. With no power, and the fundraiser due to begin in a few hours, what were they to do?

CHAPTER SIX

'I've never seen the swimming pool so full,' Monica said to Omid. Her face was flushed, and she was out of breath from running up and down sixteen flights of stairs. 'I've instructed the lifeguard to keep watch on numbers.'

Mr Walker felt puffed too. Everyone had abandoned their rooms to seek refuge in other parts of the hotel and the pool was their first stop. He'd helped Monica hand out fresh towels to guests, but the supplies had to be carried up the fire-exit stairs as the lift was out of operation. Poor Mr Walker had been run off his paws in the effort.

'Water stations have been set up on each floor and we've organised food and live music to keep guests happy,' Omid reported.

'Well done, everyone,' said Henry. 'We have no idea how long we'll be without power and we have only a few hours before the fundraiser begins, so let's just do our best to manage.'

Mr Walker caught a whiff of wet earth infused with mint and honeysuckle. *Who could that be?* He looked around and spotted a young man in

47

khaki overalls standing inside the front entrance. Mr Walker nudged Josephine's leg with his nose.

'What's up?' she asked, following his gaze. 'Oh, it's Haru, my replacement. I'd forgotten he was coming. What a day for him to begin!'

As Josephine excused herself to greet Haru, Mr Walker snuck another look at their new groundskeeper. Haru had straight black hair, kind brown eyes and a calm air about him. Despite his slight build, he appeared strong. He wore the same work boots as Josephine, which Mr Walker took as a very good sign.

Once he had been introduced, Josephine offered Haru a tour of the grounds.

'Mr Walker, perhaps you can lead the way?' she suggested. 'After all, you help a lot with the planting and maintenance of our gardens.'

Haru's eyes gleamed. 'Is that so? How charming. After you, Mr Walker.'

Mr Walker beamed with pride. He couldn't wait to show Haru the results of so much hard work. Even though many of the delicate flowers had been covered to protect them from the sun, the overall impression was of a much-loved garden brimming with colour and joy.

Suddenly, a high-pitched shriek rang out across the lawn. Mr Walker's hair stood on end. He would recognise that voice anywhere. *Sophie!*

Mr Walker raced towards the sound with Josephine and Haru hot on his trail. To everyone's relief, they found Sophie squealing with delight.

'The kids have got the right idea,' Josephine said with a wry smile.

Sophie and Amanda had set up a water sprinkler on the lawn and were playing under it with some of the children staying at the hotel.

'This is a form of *uchimizu*,' said Haru.

'*Uchimizu*?' repeated Josephine. 'What's that?'

The corners of Haru's eyes crinkled as he smiled. 'It is an ancient Japanese practice that involves sprinkling water in front of one's own house or store in the height of summer,' he explained. 'The aim is not only to eradicate dust, but to cool the temperature through heat vaporisation. *Uchimizu* was part of daily morning duties for townspeople of the Edo period. The streets of Kyoto used to be damp most of the time.'

'How fascinating,' said Josephine.

Thomas was nearby, filling one paddling pool after another with water from a hose. Mr Walker couldn't resist. He jumped into one of the pools with a great big splash.

Thomas chuckled. 'That's the first time I've ever seen you volunteer for a bath, Mr Walker.'

It was true. Mr Walker detested bath-time, but the brief respite from the heat was most welcome today. In fact, it gave Mr Walker a boost of energy. Once he

was completely and thoroughly soaked, he scampered out to join the children in a game of chasings.

CHAPTER SEVEN

M r Walker never failed to marvel at the ability of the staff to pull off the impossible. In the midst of a heatwave and a power outage, here they were greeting the first arrivals to the Guide Dogs fundraiser. Josephine and Haru had masterfully employed *uchimizu* by directing the sprinklers onto the roof of the marquee. The cascading droplets also made for a very pretty sight as they ran off the edges of the tent to create the entrancing illusion of a waterfall.

Suddenly, Mr Walker caught a familiar scent in the air: sandalwood and orange blossom. It could only be one person in the whole, wide world. His bottom waggled like jelly trifle. Mr Walker could hardly contain his excitement as Tracy Strizke, an old friend from his Guide Dog days, stepped into view. She wore a sparkly silver dress, but it was her smile that lit up Mr Walker's heart.

'Hello, my dear,' she said, enveloping him in her arms.

Mr Walker nuzzled her neck and licked both her cheeks. *Tracy! Oh, how I've missed you.*

'It's lovely to see you too.' Tracy's laugh was like a tinkling bell. 'Come,' she said, 'I have some special guests I'd like you to meet.'

The two old friends wove their way through the throng and were almost bowled over by Sophie and Amanda. The girls were bursting to meet the team from Guide Dogs, especially the puppies! While Tracy led them to the Labrador pups, Mr Walker caught up with two dogs he had trained with, who were attending the event with their owners.

People of all ages nibbled canapés and danced to the beat of the jazz band. Even the stifling heat couldn't dampen their

spirits. These guests were here to celebrate the important work Guide Dogs do, heatwave or not.

It was the smell of rain that first alerted Mr Walker. He looked up at the sky and saw dark clouds approaching from the south. He could hear the rumble of thunder in the distance and it was heading their way. He didn't like wind at the best of times and thunder hurt his ears. *Time to take cover,* thought Mr Walker.

He searched high and low for the best hiding place. Under the trees felt too exposed. The drinks table offered shelter, but the sea of glasses made him nervous. Mr Walker finally settled on the table of canapés.

Perfect! he thought, and darted underneath it.

Meanwhile, Sophie and Amanda were looking for him everywhere. They had checked with their parents, Tracy and Omid, but nobody had seen him. While pausing by the canapés to catch their breath, Amanda heard a whimper. She lifted up the tablecloth and grinned.

'There you are, Mr Walker,' she said, crawling under the table. She was joined by Amanda, and even in the dark he could see their cheeks were flushed.

'We've been looking all over for you,' Sophie said, stroking his fur. 'Oh, you're shaking.'

'Is something the matter?' Amanda's brow wrinkled with concern. 'It's not like you to stay away from a party.'

Outside, the light drizzle had morphed into big splatters of rain. The wind had picked up, and Mr Walker knew that thunder and lightning were not far off. He whined and panted heavily. He'd been afraid of thunder and lightning ever since he was a puppy. His Guide Dog training had helped him to control his fears and to look outwardly calm when frightened, but he'd never been able to quell the fear completely.

A loud crack of thunder cut through the music and hum of conversation. Mr Walker whimpered and buried his head into Sophie's lap.

Sophie's eyes widened. 'A storm! That's why Mr Walker's upset.'

'Let's get you and the puppies inside,' Amanda said.

Mr Walker reluctantly followed the girls out from under the table. The wind

howled and whipped up everything in sight. The marquee swayed from side to side. Tablecloths flapped and fluttered, spilling drinks. A lady's hat flew off into the air.

Henry and the staff set about directing the guests towards the hotel as fat drops of rain began to lash the party. The pink sunset had turned a dark grey, illuminated briefly by an angry shard of lightning.

There were squeals and whoops as the guests made a run for it. Great gusts lifted dresses and toupees and threw bow ties into a spin. One lady sank her pair of gold heels into the mud while another lost her umbrella to the howling wind.

What a disaster, thought Mr Walker. He felt terribly disappointed for Henry and the team. *The fundraiser is ruined!*

CHAPTER EIGHT

Henry and the staff immediately set about making their bedraggled guests as comfortable as possible, handing out towels and refreshments. An endless supply of lemonade was soon on hand as well as platters of sandwiches and fresh fruit, ensuring that not a single belly went hungry. So while the storm raged outdoors, the atmosphere inside the hotel was jolly. Before long, everyone had made themselves at home.

There was another flash of white as a jagged streak of lightning tore through the sky. Faces were briefly illuminated before being plunged back into the shadows of the candlelit foyer. Children shrieked with delight. Frightened puppies were comforted in willing laps. A shiver ran down Mr Walker's tail as he pressed himself closer to Mrs Reeves.

'How can we keep people's minds off the storm?' Mrs Reeves asked her daughters, who were snuggled up beside her.

'There's not much room to move around,' Sophie noted. Otherwise she would have suggested musical chairs or duck, duck, goose.

'How about we ask everyone to help make decorations for Josephine's tree?' asked Amanda.

Mrs Reeves grinned. 'Now that, little one, is a terrific idea.'

With a gleam in their eyes, the girls and Mr Walker hotfooted it up to their apartment to fetch all the materials they'd need. They returned ten minutes later and, after explaining their intention to the gathered guests, began to hand out craft materials. The response was overwhelming. Regular guests who usually kept to themselves volunteered their services and made new friends, singing Christmas carols as they worked.

Mr Walker threaded his way through the group of enthusiastic crafters. He was amazed to see how unique each and every one of the creations were. There were decorations inspired from all walks of life, from lands near and far. He paused mid-step as he overheard Sophie talking to the children.

'Our Mr Walker was a Guide Dog before he came to live with us,' she told them. 'It's a very important job that helps people who can't see very well. They assist their owners with all sorts of things, like crossing the road and getting on the bus and –'

'And cuddles,' Amanda added with a nod.

Mr Walker smiled to himself and trotted on. It was marvellous to see the many ways the power cut had brought everyone together.

Then, after much noise and carrying-on, the storm passed over. A stream of restless children poured out of the hotel doors to play outside, with Sophie and Amanda leading the charge. They jumped and stomped and plodded and splashed in the mud, making a delightful mess.

Mr Walker settled down beside Mrs Reeves. It had been an eventful day and

he was ready for a nap. He was about to close his eyes when the foyer lit up and a huge cheer rang out. The power was back on! Hooray!

CHAPTER NINE

Mr Walker had no idea how late it was, but he was certain it was well past his bedtime. And if Sophie and Amanda's yawns were any indication, it was well past theirs too.

One by one, the guests said their goodbyes. Despite the late hour, Henry and the staff were still working to ensure the hotel was spick and span in readiness for the next day.

As Chef Remy and his team handed out mugs of chocolate milk, Henry gathered everyone around for a toast.

'Congratulations to each of you for all your hard work today,' said Henry. 'We managed to pull off a successful fundraiser for a very worthy cause.'

'Indeed we did,' said Tracy, 'and I cannot thank you enough. These funds are so appreciated by our organisation. With it, we can continue to offer our clients a more independent life through the aid of a Guide Dog.'

Josephine hurried in from outside to join the others.

'Perfect timing!' Henry said. 'We have a little surprise for you.'

This was Mr Walker's cue. He trotted around the corner and lifted a paw to alert Thomas and Elvis, who wheeled in the tree now completely covered

in handmade decorations and heartfelt messages. They gently pulled to a halt in front of the assembled group. Thomas removed the trolley and the tree stood proudly, nestled in its bright red pot.

'It's beautiful!' Josephine exclaimed. 'What is it for?'

'It's a present for you, silly,' Amanda called out, giggling. After Mrs Reeves shot her a warning look, she added, 'I'm sorry. You're not silly, really.'

'For me?' Josephine clasped a hand over her mouth.

'It was a joint effort,' Henry said. 'The staff and kids and guests pitched in to make the decorations, but you'll also notice lots of special notes. It seems you have touched many hearts here at the hotel. Consider this tree as one big farewell card from us to you. I think you'll be reading it for some time.'

Josephine leaned in to read one of the messages and started laughing. 'Thanks, Elvis! I will treasure that memory also.'

There was that bittersweet feeling again, but this time Mr Walker knew that, although Josephine was leaving the hotel, she would be his friend always. She had already invited the Reeves family to visit her family farm in the school holidays and Mr Walker was looking forward to it very much. He had heard that the farm had many animal ambassadors.

Sophie appeared at her father's elbow and held up something shiny.

'Oh yes, of course.' Henry lifted Sophie into the air so she could place the tiny gold star at the top of the tree.

Mr Walker realised it was the latest piece from the advent calendar! A tiny surprise on top of a bigger surprise. It was just perfect.

As Josephine continued to read the messages and marvel at the drawings, Mr Walker remembered he still had to give her his present. He walked around the tree, sniffing the pot of soil. *Hmm, I know I put it here somewhere*, he thought. *If only I can remember exactly where . . .*

As he started to dig, the tree began to shake and wobble, sending a shower of pine needles to the floor.

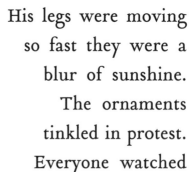

His legs were moving so fast they were a blur of sunshine. The ornaments tinkled in protest. Everyone watched on nervously as

Josephine crouched down to see what had caught his attention. 'Whatever are you doing, Mr Walker?' she asked.

Almost there, Josephine. Just one more . . . Aha! Mr Walker produced a small muddy object. He shook it free of loose dirt, then held it out to her with an air of triumph.

'Oh, thank you, Mr Walker,' she said, accepting it with a chuckle. She gave him a pat on the head. 'You shouldn't have.'

'Yes, you *really* shouldn't have,' Omid agreed, as he surveyed the big clumps of soil, pine needles and dirty paw prints which now covered the freshly mopped marble floor.

Everyone leaned in to get a better look.

Josephine wiped off the rest of the dirt and realised what it was. It was her old gardening glove – the faded red one that she and Mr Walker used for their games of tug-of-war. It was a fitting symbol of their friendship.

'Oh, Mr Walker,' she said, sniffling, 'I promised myself I wouldn't cry and now . . .' She wiped a tear from her eye. 'Come here, you.'

Josephine gave Mr Walker a big hug and everybody cheered. He inhaled her scent of rose petals and peppermint drops and let out a small, contented sigh.

'You haven't fallen asleep have you?' Josephine whispered.

Mr Walker wagged his tail. No, he was awake and enjoying every minute of being in the company of so many loved ones. He marvelled at what had turned into a most perfect day, and the knowledge that, in whatever shape or form, there were many more to come.

FRIENDS OF
MR WALKER

Mr Walker	*Labrador Ambassador*
Henry Reeves	*Hotel Manager*
Omid Abedini	*Head Concierge*
Monica Matthews	*Concierge*
Thomas Glover	*Porter*
Meraj Reddy	*Functions*
Remy Charron	*Head Chef*
Elvis Duffy	*Housekeeping*
Josephine Roberts	*Groundskeeper*
Rebecca Reeves	*Henry's wife, mother to Sophie and Amanda*
Sophie Reeves	*9-year-old daughter of Henry and Rebecca*
Amanda Reeves	*7-year-old daughter of Henry and Rebecca*
Haru	*New groundskeeper*
Tracy Strizke	*Guide Dogs Victoria*

ABOUT THE REAL MR WALKER

Born on 3 December 2015, Mr Walker was trained to provide assistance and companionship to people with low vision or blindness by Guide Dogs Victoria. After achieving many milestone stages in his training, it was decided that his larger-than-life personality was best suited to an ambassador role, where his affectionate nature would truly be able to shine.

Under the principal care of the hotel manager, who is also his official foster carer, Mr Walker has been calling Park Hyatt Melbourne home since 2017. Mr Walker quickly made a name for himself within the hotel as well as with the wider Melbourne community through daily meet-and-greets in the hotel lobby. He has rubbed shoulders with people from all walks of life, including celebrities, and even achieved his own celebrity status when *The Project* caught wind of the four-legged ambassador and aired him on their evening news.

Despite his rise to fame, Mr Walker prefers to spend most of his time within the hotel's serene grounds, nestled between parklands and elm-lined boulevards. His gentle nature shines most when he is greeting guests with a warm, furry welcome and making everyone at the hotel feel right at home.

ABOUT GUIDE DOGS AUSTRALIA

Every hour of every day, an Australian family learns that their loved one will have severe or permanent sight-loss. Nine of these Australians will eventually go blind. It is estimated that there are over 450,000 Australians who are blind or have low vision and this number is expected to significantly increase with an ageing population.

Guide Dogs Australia, in collaboration with its state-based organisations, delivers essential services to children, teenagers and the elderly who are blind or have low vision in every state and territory across Australia. Their mission is to assist people who are blind or have low vision to gain the freedom and independence to move safely and confidently around their communities, and to fulfil their potential.

For more information about Guide Dogs Australia, visit guidedogsaustralia.com.au

Jess Black is an Australian author of children's books. She has written over thirty junior fiction books and two picture books, *Moon Dance* and *The Bold Australian Girl*. Jess is the author of the Keeper of the Crystals series and the Guide Dogs Australia Little Paws series, and is the co-author of the hugely successful Bindi Wildlife Adventure series and the RSPCA Animal Tales series.

Sara Acton is an award-winning author and illustrator of children's books. She lives on the Central Coast of New South Wales with one husband, two children, a mischievous dog and a cat called Poppy, who's definitely in charge.

Can't get enough of Mr Walker?
Collect the series!

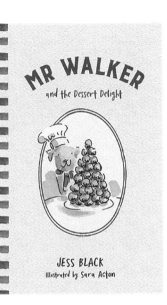

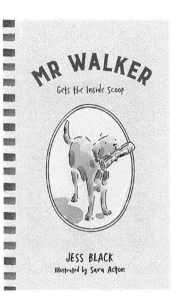

See how it all began in

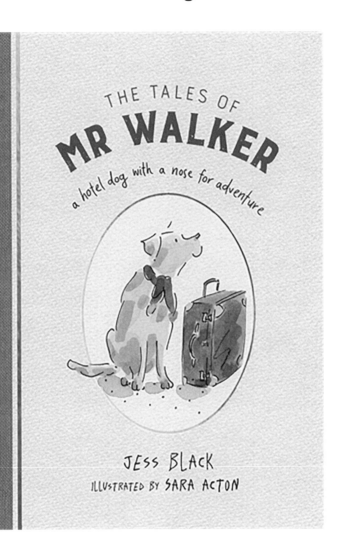

THE TALES OF

MR WALKER

a hotel dog with a nose for adventure

JESS BLACK

ILLUSTRATED BY SARA ACTON

Available now